THE BOOK NO ONE SHOULD OPEN

SCARY STORIES

HORROR ANTHOLOGY

Published by NR Evans Studio LLC
© 2024

The Book No One Should Open:
Scary Stories Horror Anthology
Text copyright © 2024 by N.R. Evans
Illustrations copyright © 2024 by N.R. Evans
All rights reserved. No part of this book may be
used or reproduced in any manner without
written permission except in the case of brief quotations
embodied in critical articles and reviews.
For information email
N.R.EvansStudio@gmail.com

ISBN: 979-8-9905252-1-4 (epub)
ISBN 979-8-9905252-0-7 (pbk.)

*To my beloved family
past, present, and future*

Contents

- Ghosts Are Everywhere -

Some people believe ghosts are souls of the dead, or chaotic moments from the past echoing through the ages. Others theorize that ghosts are evil spirits old as time itself, or beings from another plane of existence who cross into our world. It's said they sense our fear and anxiety, drawing power from it. It's even been hypothesized that ghosts could be psychic phenomena manifested by the human mind.

Whatever ghosts are, they've been recorded in eyewitness accounts throughout history. One needn't travel far to find places reportedly haunted by restless spirits who wander lonely corridors and empty rooms. Some place close to you, likely even in your own hometown, will have a reputation for ghost sightings or other paranormal manifestations. From ghostly ships on the high seas to phantom hitchhikers on deserted highways, ghosts are everywhere.

A Feeling of Dread

It was late at night and David Bradley was fast asleep. He awakened suddenly, with an intense feeling of dread.

He expected to see a blank ceiling above him. Instead, he saw a pale and ghastly face only inches from his own. Staring at him wide-eyed, its jaws gaping open, it remained nearly motionless, locked in its frightful expression.

David was paralyzed with fear. He stared in blood-curdling horror at the deeply sunken eyes flicking back and forth within its head. The hazy thing hovered over him, grinding long, yellowed teeth as if it were chewing gristle.

The sound of its gnashing was awful, and thunderous in David's ears. It sent a violent chill through his body. He jerked the blanket over himself and held it there firmly, trembling in terror. The sound drifted slowly towards the foot of his bed.

As he clutched his covers, he felt it gently *pulling* at them. He held tighter, horrified as it began forcefully tearing his blanket away. David struggled and fought, screaming like a banshee.

The thing fought harder still, and David could not hold on. His covers slipped through

his fingers and were snatched away, leaving him curled in a shrieking ball on his bed.

When his parents burst into the room, they turned on the light and the thing vanished.

"What's wrong? Are you okay?"

"There's something in here!" David cried, as his mother took him into her arms. "It pulled my covers off!"

His father searched the closet, under the bed, and inside a laundry basket, but found nothing.

"It was just a nightmare," he said. "Let's tuck you in and get back to sleep."

He picked up the blanket from the floor and gently laid it over David, still sniffling in his bed. His mother let out a frightened gasp. At the foot of the blanket, burned into the fabric, were two charred, blackened handprints.

The Wallet

Driving through the country on a moonless night, Richard Creely saw something small, black, and rectangular on the side of the road. He abruptly stopped the car, reversed, and drove back to the spot. There on the ground was a trifold wallet next to a busted utility pole.

He got out of the car, picked up the wallet, and looked it over. It was dirty, and there was a weathered $100 bill inside, along with an old, faded driver's license.

Pleased with his find, he brushed it off and placed it in his front pocket, then returned to his car and continued on his way.

About a mile down the road Richard realized he was not alone. Someone was sitting in the back seat. Alarmed, he asked them who they were and how they got there.

"My name is Gary Allen. I was driving down this road and I saw a wallet lying on the shoulder. I stopped and picked it up, then a man appeared in my back seat, and told me he'd also stopped and found the wallet. Then he did this."

The stranger leaned forward, grabbed the steering wheel, and jerked it hard to the right. The car veered sharply and crashed into a utility pole.

When Richard finally came to his senses, he

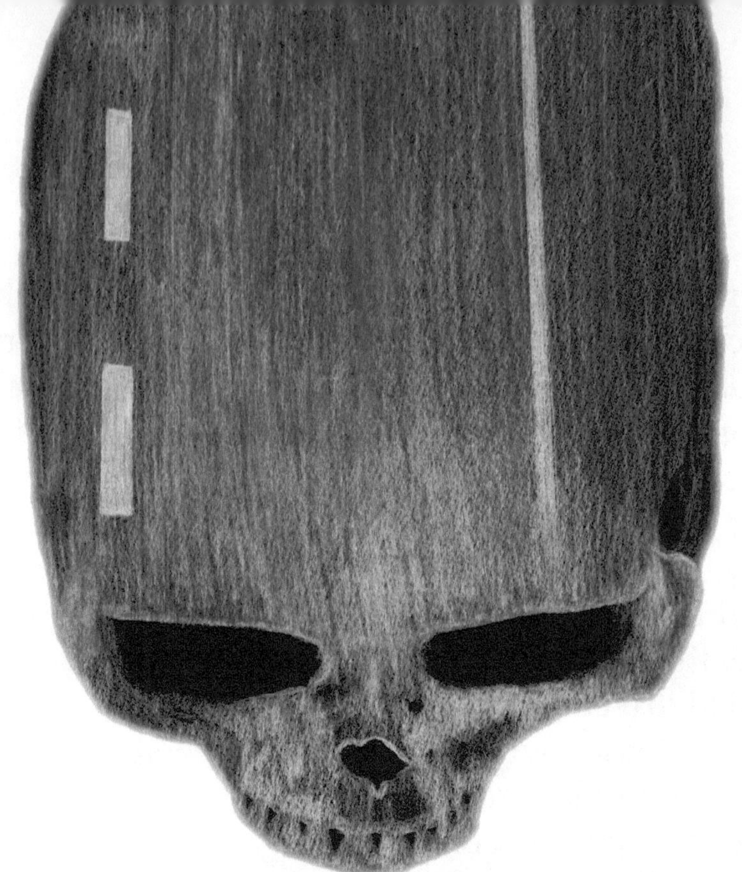

was sitting in the back seat of someone else's old sedan, and a man he had never seen before was driving.

"Who are you?" the man asked in a frightened voice.

"My name is Richard Creely. I was driving down this road when I saw a wallet in my headlights. I stopped and picked it up, and a man appeared in my back seat. He told me he'd also picked up the wallet once. Then he did this." Richard's ghost said, reaching for the steering wheel...

The Sandstorm

A man was running a long-distance race through the desert when a sandstorm moved in like a pride of roaring lions. It was so powerful he couldn't see the road ahead, or even his hand in front of his face.

Race officials had warned this could happen. They told everyone if it did, not to move until the sandstorm passed. He couldn't resist the urge to just keep going and win it all while everyone else huddled for shelter.

Though blinded by sand, he was sure he knew which direction to go. He felt what he thought was the path underfoot, so he kept pushing forward.

For hours the storm scraped and battered everything in its way, and when it finally passed, he was so exhausted and thirsty he couldn't even swallow. The storm had blotted out the sun, but now it blazed mercilessly above him in the bright blue sky. He looked around for the road but couldn't see it anywhere. He had no idea where he was.

The man continued walking for miles beneath cloudless skies, dragging his feet and dreaming of cool water. In the distance, he spotted a small shrub; it was the only shade as far as the eye could see. He walked for what seemed like ages until he arrived there. Exhausted and filthy,

he collapsed in its shadow.

With no idea how long he'd been there, he awoke to the sound of a pickup truck driving in the distance. He jumped up and began running, waving his arms and shouting to get their attention. The red truck suddenly turned in his direction.

'I'm saved!' he thought. 'They see me!'

The truck sped closer. As it approached, he was still waving his arms, but it wasn't slowing. He jumped out of the way as the truck roared past him. It drove straight to the lone shrub where he laid only minutes ago.

He approached the pickup, shouting, "Hey! I'm right here! What are you doing? Hello?"

Two men stepped out and stood with their backs to him. Neither paid him any attention. They just shifted uneasily, staring underneath the bush. He tried to see what they were looking at, but they were blocking his view. Finally, one of them spoke.

"I don't know why; I just suddenly had this feeling we'd find him here."

"It's a real shame we were too late," the other man replied.

Janice McMannis

Remember ol' Janice McMannis?
(The girl from the back of the class,
by the map of the world?)
At recess she always seemed normal to me,
But Joey and Jessica both disagree.
She simply sat down on the bench one day,
And never got up again to play.
We asked her if she needed anything but,
She never replied, and she never looked up.
When recess was over, we all went inside.
"Ol' Janice is still on the bench!" someone cried.
The teacher said, "Janice McMannis, get up!"
Yet still she remained on the bench, like a lump.
The teacher reached out, just to lift up her head..
And it fell off cause' Janice McMannis was dead!

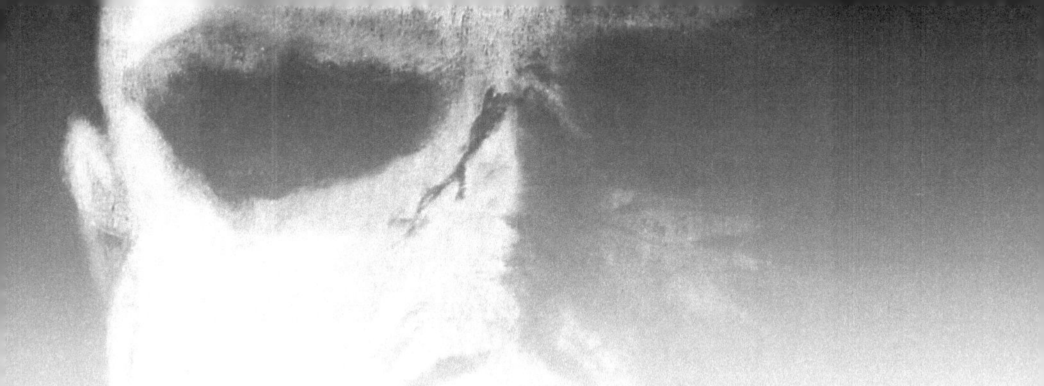

The Thing from the Streets

Will lived in the city. The sidewalks, rooftops, and alleyways were his backyard.

One day, while exploring a brick alley far from home, he came upon a corpse in a dumpster among the bags of trash. The corpse had clearly been there for a while and was in awful shape. Its lips peeled back in a gruesome sort of "smile". The flesh was all shades of blue, brown, and yellow where it showed from tattered clothes. Swarming flies buzzed loudly.

When Will saw it, he was so frightened that he ran all the way home, and didn't stop to tell anyone what he'd seen. He tried not to think about it, but he couldn't help it. What was he doing there? Did he fall in there by accident? Did something get him? Will didn't know, and wasn't sure that he even wanted to. He knew he should tell the police, but was afraid they'd think he had something to do with it.

That night at dinner, he didn't even tell his parents. If they found out just how far he'd strayed from home they'd never let him explore the city again. He just wanted to forget it, so he kept putting it out of his mind as he watched tv, brushed his teeth, and laid in bed. Eventually, Will closed his eyes and drifted off to sleep.

"You left me," said a gravelly voice in the darkness of Will's room.

Will awakened and sat up, his eyes opened wide, trying to see in the dim moonlight. He wasn't sure if he had dreamed the voice, until it spoke again.

"You left me out there all alone."

His blood ran cold. "No!" he whimpered, then held his breath, listening intently. There were flies buzzing, but he still couldn't see anything.

"Yes, you saw me, and you left me. You can't just walk away from me," said the voice as something big leaned into his doorway.

When he heard sharp metal scratching at the wooden doorframe, his heart jumped into his throat. Will squeezed his eyes shut and ducked under his blanket. The scraping sound moved across the far wall, turned the corner, and continued toward his bed. As it traveled around the room, Will's pulse beat faster and faster.

The sound stopped right next to him. After

a long silence, he peeked out from under the blanket, glimpsing himself in the mirror. Also in the reflection, sticking out from underneath his bed, was the corpse. It was even more ghastly than the last time he'd seen it.

"You'll know how it feels to live alone among garbage," it said, disappearing into the darkness beneath his bed.

Will's brain, having been temporarily frozen with fear, suddenly screamed *'run!'*, prompting him to leap all the way from his mattress through the open doorway. He landed in the hall and sprinted towards his parents' room.

"Mom! Dad! The thing from the streets is following me!" he yelled in a panic, bounding through their door.

Despite all the commotion, neither of them so much as moved in the bed. Will pulled back the blanket, and he screamed as a swarm of flies poured out from underneath. His parents were gone, and in their place were bags of trash.

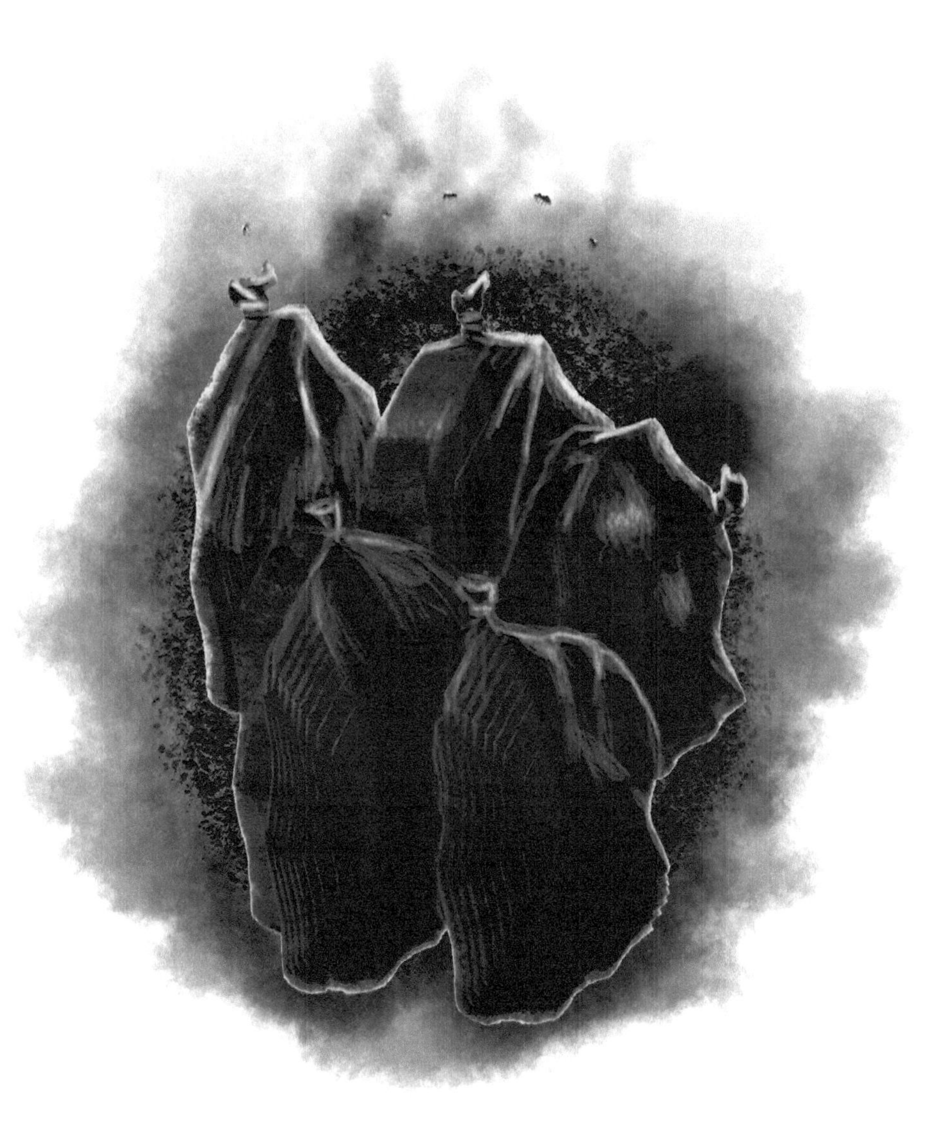

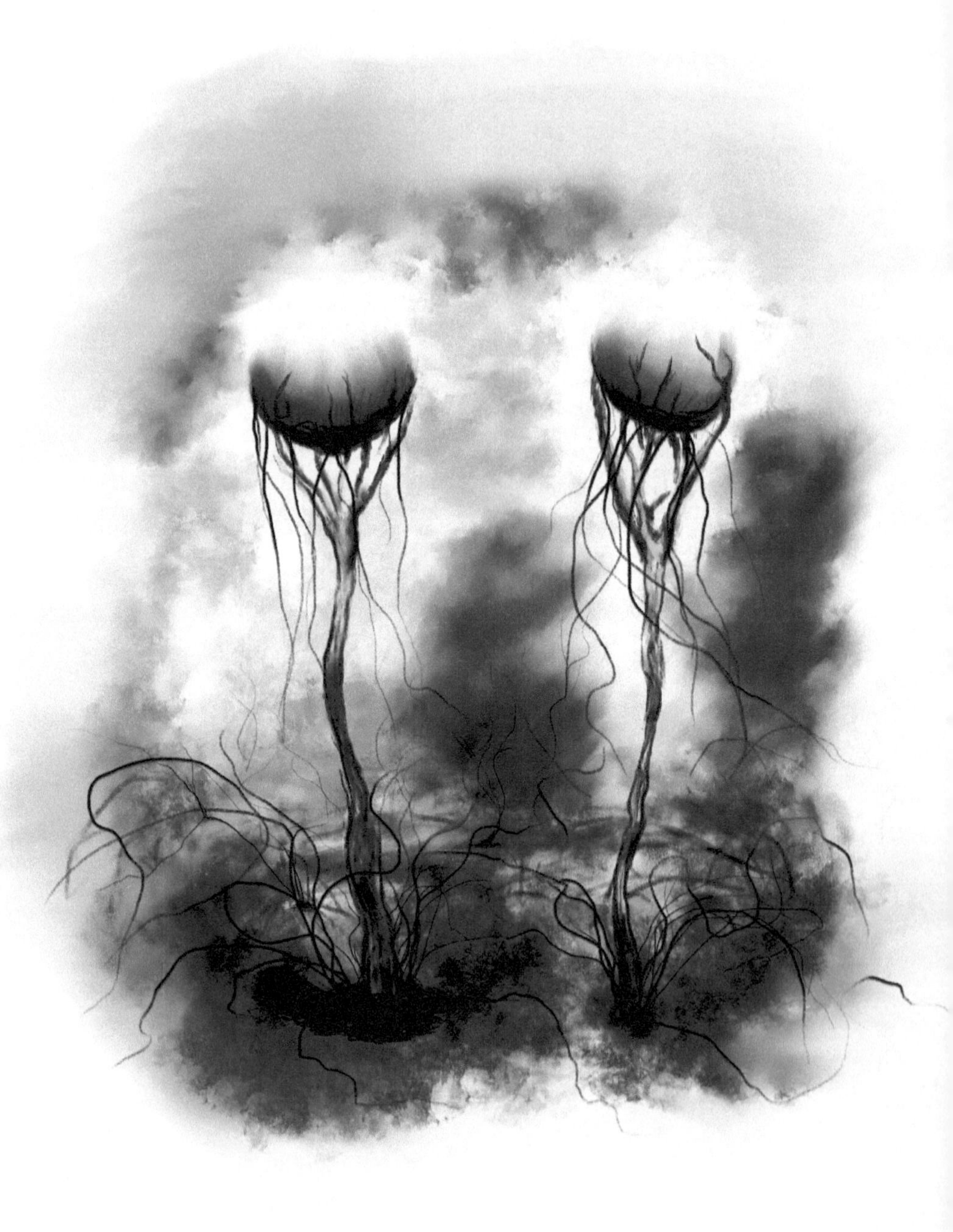

Things Aren't Always What They Seem

*O*ur minds are terribly susceptible to being deceived, deluded, duped, misled, mistaken, misinformed, misguided, swindled, snookered, kidded, conned, suckered, bluffed, and often they're just plain wrong.

For instance, there are significant blind spots in human vision, which your brain simply fills with information it makes up as it goes along. Anything could be there, in the corner of your eye, hiding right next to you. You'd never even know.

The Faerie Ring

Maya and Sofia were staying with their grandmother while their parents were away. She was a gentle old woman, and the girls' parents instructed them to be on their best behavior. They soon found themselves misbehaving anyway.

First, they set a towel on fire playing with the stove. Then they broke the neighbor's window throwing rocks and lied about it. When questioned, they loudly blamed each other until they were screaming insults back and forth.

"Enough!" said their grandmother. "I am too old to make you girls behave! You must have some self-control! Tomorrow you will do the chores you've been neglecting and there will be no more arguing! Do you understand?"

"Yes," said the girls, their heads hung low.

When the next day arrived, they ran out without doing any chores. They walked through the creek and into the woods to search for the witch's house that a woodcutter's boy had warned them about.

"The witch who lives in the clearing is the least of it," he'd explained. "Evil is everywhere in those woods. You'd be wise to stay out of them."

Soon, the girls spotted the clearing and a large, windowless hut. It was made of crooked branches and sticky, black pitch, with a straw-thatched roof. They didn't enter the clearing, but lurked hidden in the woodline, gazing upon the strange house. Thick, black smoke billowed from the chimney. They began trying to pelt the hut with stones.

"Have you come to see the witch?" asked a voice behind them. Startled, they turned to find a girl their age in a brown cloak. She had long, black hair that flowed from beneath her hood. "I'm sorry to tell you, but no one has ever seen her."

"We came to see the house, and now we have, so we'll just be going," said Maya.

"Wait, don't go yet! Don't you want to see the faerie ring?"

The girls didn't know what a faerie ring was, but they were interested in finding out.

"Come on," she said, leading them into the clearing. "It's right over here."

They approached a large circle of toadstools on the ground, at least 10 feet across. The black-haired girl smiled and asked them if they could hear the music, but they could not.

"Listen closely," she said. When the girls did, they faintly detected the most beautiful melodies their ears had ever heard. They closed their eyes and swayed, enchanted by the tune.

"If you wish to see the faeries, you just step

into the ring."

Maya and Sofia already felt a strange longing to enter the circle, as if some unseen force beckoned them. At the girl's suggestion, they could no longer resist the urge, and both stepped inside.

Immediately, they found themselves dancing round and round, surrounded by faeries frolicking, laughing, and smiling as they twirled each other joyously. The faint music had grown loud, almost deafening now. The faeries and festivities had been invisible from outside the ring, but now enveloped all their senses.

The enchanting music quickened as the faeries played faster. Their tiny faces were no longer jolly and inviting, though. Their smiles had transformed into evil grins, gritted with malice. Maya and Sofia were dancing with such fervor, they failed to even notice. They grew tired but couldn't stop themselves; on and on they danced. Their feet hurt, they were out of breath, and they were frightened. They didn't know what was happening to them.

The young girl with black hair was still outside the circle, giggling, then laughing, until her laugh grew into a cackle. She grew taller, ageing years in a matter of moments. Suddenly, there stood a wrinkled, old crone with grey hair, wrapped in the brown cloak. She had tricked the

girls, for anyone who steps into a faerie ring is cursed to dance forever.

"If you don't control yourselves," she

sneered, hobbling back to her hut, "someone else will."

An Insufferable Creature

Hector Venegas had nightmares for weeks, and they were only getting worse.

"You'll be alright, dear," his mother assured him as he readied himself for bed. "Bad dreams can't hurt you."

Hector wasn't so sure. He'd been having terrible headaches and was tired all the time. When he looked in the mirror he saw dark circles under his eyes and small bruises around his head. He knew it had something to do with the nightmares.

Hector laid down, and after drifting off to sleep, he began to dream. He found himself alone on a deserted city street, surrounded by abandoned shops and carts. The pavement cooked beneath the scorching sun, and the only sound was the gusting wind, tousling his black hair.

In the distant, wavy haze over the roadway, a car appeared. It drew closer, and Hector saw it was a long, black hearse. The hair stood up on his neck as the hearse rolled to a stop beside him. He gulped nervously, and the tinted window lowered, revealing the specter that had been haunting all of Hector's dreams: The headless man.

CLANG! A bell sounded loudly and startled him. He spun around to find he was standing before a church. When he looked up, he saw a girl in the bell tower waving a bright red scarf.

CLANG! The bell sounded again, and the girl cupped her hands to her mouth, shouting something. Hector could faintly hear her; what was she saying?

"Waake uuup, Hector! Waaaaake uuuup!"

Hector awoke in his room to find a horrid, pale creature sitting on his chest, its jaws stretched wide around his head. He screamed, pushing with all his might at its bony, withered form. The gaping mouth slipped off, and the screeching creature was thrown against the wall, flailing the repulsive, writhing stumps that must have been legs. Hector was still screaming as it frantically up-righted itself, scampered out the open door and disappeared into the hallway. He backed into the corner, terrified.

When his mother came into the room, he hastily explained what had happened. She insisted it was only a nightmare, but Hector swore it was real.

The next day, Hector's grandmother came to visit. "Hector, my little angel, you don't look well! Come, tell me, what's wrong?"

He explained everything- the creature, the nightmares, and his mother's disbelief.

"I believe you Hector," she said, untying a faded red scarf from around her head and revealing a set of strange scars. "I too encountered this thing as a child. It feeds on your good thoughts, leaving only the bad ones behind. It is a weak, insufferable creature. It can only hurt you if you fear it. Do not be afraid! You must imagine standing up for yourself and destroying it. When the monster eats *that* good thought, it will become so fearful of you it will never return."

That night Hector dreamed he was back on the abandoned city street. He saw the hearse approaching and felt the fear rising inside of him, but he stood his ground. As the window lowered and revealed the man with no head, Hector called out, "You don't scare me! I know what you are!"

The man began convulsing, then shriveled up until he became the leathery little monster from his room. Hector opened the car door, and the creature fell out, flopping harmlessly at his feet. Its awful mouth opened and closed, like a fish out of water.

"This is *my* dream!" he said, bringing his foot down onto it with such force that it splattered. The putrid remains sizzled and belched smoke, then were gone.

A cry of joy rang out. He looked up to see the girl with the bright red scarf in the bell tower smiling down upon him with pride.
Hector waved and smiled back, finally recognizing who she was.

A Long Walk in the Dark

Steven lost track of time playing at a friend's house. Before he knew it, night had fallen, and he slipped out into the chilled autumn air to hurry home. The streetlights cast pale circles on the dark pavement.

His neighborhood looked different at night, desolate and hostile. The dead leaves chattered furiously in the breeze and crunched beneath his shoes. The trees shuddered as the cold wind howled through their spindly branches.

Steven felt his fear beginning to grow. Each storm drain promised doom within its murky recesses. Every house seemed to loom over him like some ancient monster. He was almost certain that something was stalking him from the shadows. He tried his best to watch every direction at once.

Something in the distance caught his eye, and he froze in his tracks, staring hard. Several blocks behind him on the black asphalt was an inky, fluttering shape, crawling low and fast. It raised up tall for a moment, standing like a man, then contorted itself sideways, snaking back to the ground and undulating toward Steven.

His eyes bulged, and horror washed over him. He immediately turned around to walk *much* faster.

He was only a block from home now. He was

telling himself he'd just imagined it, as he looked back a second time. The street appeared empty, but it was hard to see. He stopped, his eyes straining in the darkness.

The thing reemerged closer still, flashing quickly into the glow of another streetlight only a block behind. A gust of wind surged and he lost track of the glistening phantom as it charged into the darkness once more.

Now Steven was running. He knew it would catch up to him in only a matter of moments. He glanced back mid-stride and there, only 20 feet behind him, was the tattered, hooded specter, not crawling but *flying* inches above the ground as it rapidly approached.

Steven's heart pounded in his chest, and he ran harder than he'd ever run before. He could see his driveway now and began shouting for help as he sprinted. When he looked back one last time, his screams were instantly muffled as the shape took flight with impossible speed and wrapped him in darkness.

Steven fell hard, tumbling along the ground. He reached up, frantically peeling the thing from his face. In his hands he held a tattered trash bag, flapping in the wind.

Skeleton Surprise

Twelve skeletons in a big black pot,
Stewed and simmered in thick, brown broth.
Ladle me some while it's nice and hot..
Thirteen skeletons in a black pot!

A Strange and Terrible Sound

There were six of us in the lifeboat after the storm overturned our cargo ship. We were thousands of miles from home and hundreds of miles from land. Deepest, bluest ocean rose and fell in every direction as far as the eye could see.

At first, we looked for more survivors, but it was no use; the ocean giveth and the ocean taketh away. Two men argued which direction would take us to land, until I reminded them that without any oars or a sail, we were adrift at the mercy of the waves.

It wasn't long before the sun slipped below the horizon, and we were left in total darkness out there on that cold, black ocean.

As we lay in a heap, shivering in the misty night air, something strange and terrible sounded way out on those endless waves. I felt compelled to raise my head the first time I heard it, and I looked out over the sea shimmering in the moonlight. I couldn't see anything, and I lay back down, listening. Moments later it sounded again, much closer and much louder, and all of us were looking around now.

"What was that?" one man asked, fearfully.

"Is it another survivor adrift? It almost sounded human!" exclaimed another.

"Cover your ears or that'll be the last sound you ever hear," barked Greeves, the oldest man among us. He clasped his hands over his ears, clearly shaken. "Almost human is right, in the same way that a lure is almost a fish, or a decoy is almost a duck. That sound is a siren come up from the deep to feed on the shipwreck. If you fancy your lives you won't listen to that song! It'll take you to your graves!"

I clasped my hands over my ears, too. I don't think I believed in monsters before, but out there adrift on the dark ocean, that old sailor who had seen more than I could ever imagine suddenly becoming so afraid, made *me* very afraid.

The world was dreamlike in the silence of my muted hearing. The old man's face looked anguished as his lips continued to move pleadingly. The men he was shouting at looked baffled and amused, and then annoyed as Greeves kept calling his warning.

Suddenly, they jerked their heads to the starboard side in unison, and I knew they had heard it again. The old man had gone from just shouting to kicking their legs frantically to get their attention, but none of the sailors even flinched. They stared slack-jawed, in awe at what they saw—the source of the hypnotic sound.

No more than 30 yards away rose the most

horrible thing I've ever seen. A ghastly head, shoulders, and then torso slowly extruded from the water, facing the lifeboat. At first glance it looked to be a woman with long black hair, but even at such a distance something appeared very wrong.

Her wide eyes didn't blink as she stared directly at us. That hideous face didn't move or change, as if it were painted on. Her arms dangled lifelessly at her sides as she swayed to and fro, like a rubbery puppet propped up on a stick. Her skin was pale with a bluish tint, but suddenly became dark green at waist level. Slimy, and tubular, like an eel or a hagfish, this "fish tail" extended into the frothing waves.

Quick as lightning, all four of those sailors were over the starboard side and into that black, endless deep. The old man and I were screaming at them to get back into the lifeboat, but it was no use; their minds were not their own. They were swimming out to meet their doom with open arms. Wide smiles stretched across their faces as they paddled frantically.

When they were halfway between the boat and the "mermaid", she began rapidly rising above the waves, high into the air. The eel-like stalk of her tail was shooting up out of the water, revealing her to be as tall as a palm tree against the black sky awash in stars.

I watched in horror as the moonlight revealed a face the size of a barn looming just beneath them. It lunged ravenously, whipping the water into a frenzy as it broke the surface, its mouth wide, revealing hundreds of gleaming teeth the length of harpoons. It swallowed the four sailors all at once. The titanic jaws snapped shut and its massive, horrible visage sank into the ocean foam. The stalk extending from its forehead lowered back into the deep, and the "mermaid" lure on the end slipped silently beneath the waves.
For three days Greeves and I covered our ears with our hands, exhausted and on the brink of death, praying we'd be rescued.

It is now the fourth day, and I have awakened to a strange and wonderful sound! I look to discover there is a maiden of the fairest beauty, beckoning us with the voice of an angel, to come and meet with her. The old man is already swimming out to her as I dive off the boat into the deep blue waves. The vast ocean is all around me, and miles below me as I swim out to.. as I swim out to… what was I doing again?

(Pause momentarily, then jump at your nearest friend and scream, "AAHHH!" like you're being eaten by a giant fish).

The Spaces Between Time Itself

This world was once void and without form, bathed in complete darkness, and crawling with unspeakable evil. Oceans of it rose and fell like mountains and everything was lost in the waves before it had even begun.

Then came the light, cutting millions of miles across space, from all around, banishing the evil to the dark recesses where light's glow does not touch; to the shadows, to the underground, and to the spaces between time itself.

Eons passed as the war between light and darkness raged on. The light brought life, and the darkness brought about its death, and the cycle continued without end. When the heavens would align, and the moon eclipsed the sun, evil would spill out into the day. It seethed up and exploded from mountains. In the black clouds of ash, the evil would thrive and destroy everything it touched. When the skies filled with darkness, more evil bubbled forth from the trenches and crevices of the abyss, to drag all the life it could manage back into the depths.

Still, the ash would eventually settle, and the light would crack the sky again to reach the world, eternally chasing the darkness around the earth, creating night and day. While the evil was kept at bay, life survived and flourished.

The light created new ways to manifest itself, but so too did the darkness. Shadowy forests became places where evil could prowl. It moved across deserts in great, chaotic storms of sand and raged across seas within whirling hurricanes. Eventually, with the arrival of humans, evil found a way inside of life itself, as the vastness of human imagination gave it infinite room to grow.

The evil influenced humanity to build it more

places to dwell in the outside world- beneath roofs, behind walls, in the sewers, basements, cellars, attics, dungeons, and tombs of our world. Under our beds and our floorboards, in the shadowy corners of our closets and crawlspaces where the light never touches, is evil as old as time waiting impatiently all around us. It has no other want or purpose than to drag us, kicking and screaming, back into the void from whence we came.

Like the tides that ebb and flow in time with the moon, it is not a question of if, but when- when will the evil rise again? When will the darkness surge across the land? When will it come for you?

1313

Sharlene often had an uneasy feeling in her home at 1313 Parish Road. The shadows under the staircase, the dark doorways, empty rooms, and foul depths of the decrepit cellar gave her nightmares places to live and room to grow.

She would hear footsteps and whispers. Random doors creaked open and slammed shut. Ghastly things emerged in the corner of her eye, but when she turned to look, they were gone- shapes moving in the darkness, faces that disappeared before she could catch a glimpse.

"My mind must be playing tricks on me," she would tell herself.

Sharlene eventually got used to it, or ignored it for being unpleasant, as people often do. One day her Aunt Bernice came to visit, and she brought with her a friend who she introduced as a psychic medium.

"This is Charles. He communicates with people who have passed on," Aunt Bernice said. The man politely shook Sharlene's hand and followed her inside. His easy smile and relaxed demeanor instantly faded as he crossed the threshold into Sharlene's living room.

"There's something in here" he said with great interest, his gleaming eyes scanning around.

"Just a lot of old furniture" Sharlene said.

"I don't mean an object," he said, unwinding the scarf from his neck. "I mean an entity."

Sharlene laughed nervously, though it came out as more of a whimper. She was suddenly pale with fear. This medium had walked in, and in no time confirmed what she had denied to herself for all these months; she was not alone in her house.

"I knew it! I told you I felt something in here!" Aunt Bernice exclaimed, pulling out three chairs at the dining room table. "Let's speak with it!"

"Oh, yes!" Charles eagerly agreed. "Let's find out why they're here and what they want! Maybe we could assist them in moving on, and you could have your house to yourself."

The pressure of both their gazes fell upon Sharlene, who reluctantly replied, "Oh, well... alright then. If you think it could work."

Bernice rushed to shut off the lights. Around the table they gathered there in the dark, around a single candle, joining hands in a circle.

"Tonight, we wish to speak with the one who dwells among us," Charles began. "We beckon you, come out from the shadows, we mean you no harm."

The air in the room became thin and cold, and the candle's flame burned red as blood. A dry whisper like an ancient corpse's voice announced, "We cannot come out from the shadows. We do not hide in the darkness and watch you; we are the darkness itself."

"...What is your name?" Charles asked suspiciously. A still silence hung for a moment, followed by the sound of someone drawing a deep breath.

The windows blasted open as a furious wind overtook the room. Countless voices called out so many names at once it sounded like screeching white noise. Everyone grimaced and squeezed each other's hands. Dust fell from the ceiling as it shook with the sound, but stopped as suddenly as it began. Startled, they looked around at one another in the momentary silence.

The voice spoke again, this time roaring with contempt.

"You hide behind your eyes, for now, looking out upon the realm which only eyes can see. We have no eyes and cannot see it. We have no tongues and cannot taste it. We have no hands and cannot touch it. We've lost our minds and cannot remember it!"

Horrible, scathing laughter filled the room.

"We wait, still and silent. We are the darkness you will always fear, and our time shall come again! Like mirrors facing mirrors, we go on forever."

"You certainly do," said Charles hastily as he released their hands, pushed his chair back, and rose to his feet. The candle's flame returned to a yellow hue, and he blew it out abruptly.

"What happened?" Bernice asked, looking puzzled as Charles wrapped the scarf back around his neck, preparing to leave.

"Why did we stop?"

"Dearest Bernice, I talk to the dead." he began, opening the front door. His face was pale and gravely serious. "Whatever that was just declared it was not human, that it hadn't really been alive to begin with, and perhaps even suggested that it cannot die. I do not talk to the darkness itself, that is absolute madness. I suggest we all leave this place at once before we find out what something with no eyes, tongue, or hands could possibly even want, or what it's capable of. Sharlene, thank you for having me. It was nice meeting you, but I must be going. Bernice, it was good to see you again, but I cannot stay here another minute."

With that, he shuddered and closed the door behind him. The two women looked at one another, then quickly followed suit.

Sharlene sold the house and moved out of state. The darkness itself stayed as promised, forever awaiting the universe's inevitable return to its first and most essential form, void of all light and warmth... but that is a story for another time.

Nothing Out of the Ordinary

For George Willis, today had been like any other day. He awoke, had cereal for breakfast, rode the bus to school, and played baseball in the park. Later, he ate dinner, then got ready for his bath—nothing out of the ordinary. He turned on the hot water, filled the tub, and climbed in. Even his bath seemed perfectly unremarkable.

George had just finished washing with soap, and the clear water had become cloudy and grey. He lathered his hair with shampoo then plunged his head beneath the surface.

At once, George knew he was no longer in

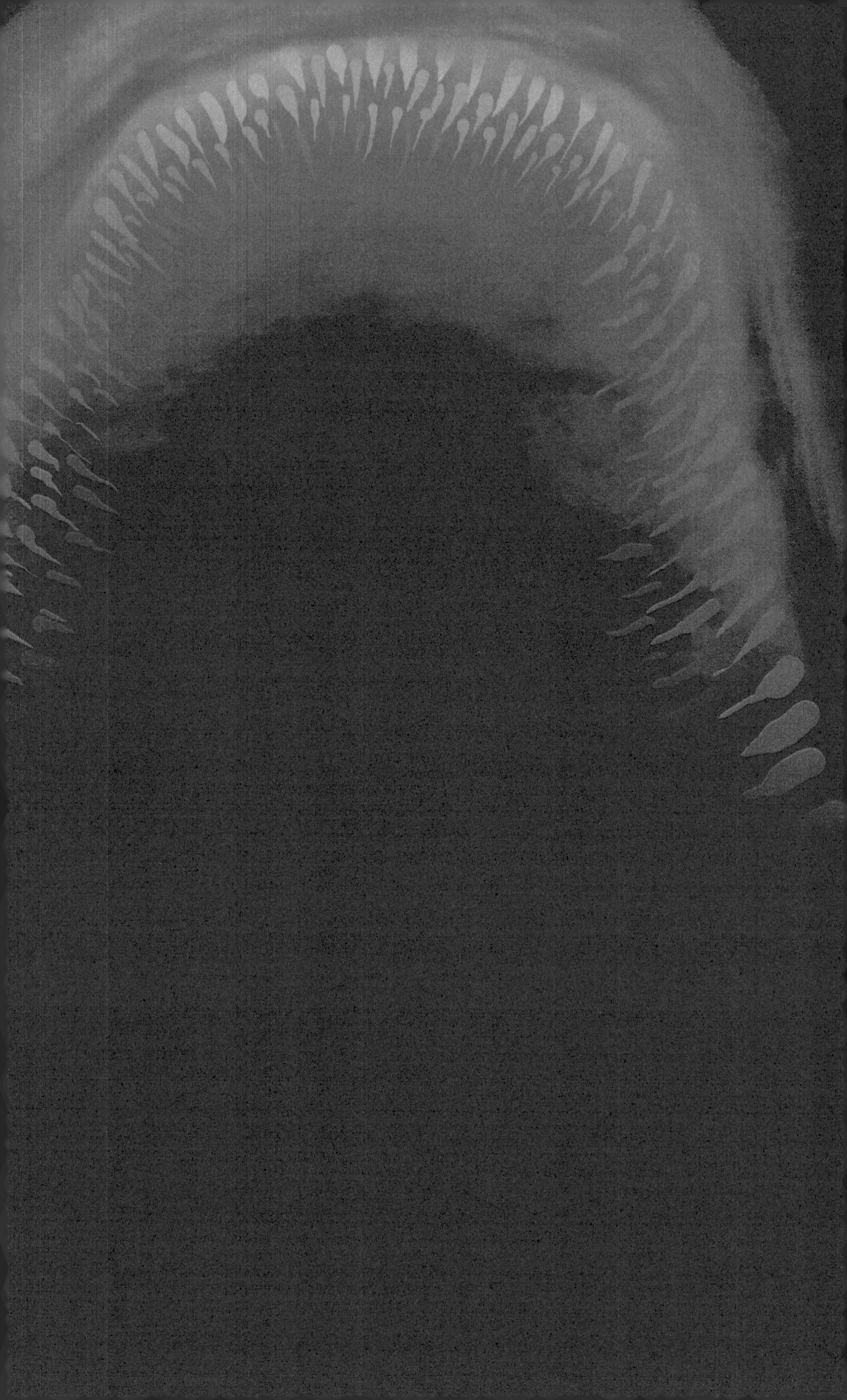

his tub at home. When his head went underwater, he was somehow transported to the middle of a deep, vast swamp, surrounded by slimy logs and twisted branches that rose from its depths.

He tried to find the surface in his panic, but he couldn't. He reached out and touched something huge, leathery, and alive. It growled, rolling over next to George. He screamed.

Air bubbles escaped his mouth, and he thought quickly. George stuck his hand out to feel which direction the stream of bubbles travelled, then followed them as fast as he could.

He sensed something big was approaching from below in the deep water. He kicked and flailed with all he had. It was coming! In his mind he could see its huge mouth opening wide to clamp down on his legs with razor sharp teeth and drag him into the abyss.

He was out of breath and out of time. The world was growing dark, as points of light danced behind his eyelids. Still thrashing, he knew it's jaws were closing around him. He broke the surface of the water, and gasped loudly for air.

Opening his eyes, George saw he was right back in his own bathtub. Relieved that it had just been his imagination, he sat wiping his face. George leaned forward, reached for the drain plug, and disappeared with barely a ripple.

A New Arrival

I used to have hair that was pretty and clean,
And ruby red lips that would part when I'd smile.
I used to be able to blink with my eyes,
But that was all back when I was alive.
My skin is all sallow and runny beneath,
My lips and my gums pulled away from my teeth.
My eyes are both bulging and stuck open wide,
Nothing like back when I was alive.
There isn't much down here,
but darkness and dirt,
The worms and the smell of decay.
I've been awful lonely for quite a long time,
But all of that's over... now that you've arrived!

Everyday Horrors

We needn't look far to find fearfully fascinating stories to frighten your mind and send terror piercing through your heart. People live each and every day in close proximity to the dreadful and the macabre. We barely stop to pay it any mind, until it inevitably comes tumbling into our laps. It's almost like we're all just ignoring it, hoping it won't happen to us.

The Rental

Mira moved out of her parents' house and was living on her own for the first time. She leased an apartment on the top floor of an old building. No one could get into the windows that high up, she thought. Also, no one would be above her, banging and booming. More importantly, it was half the price of the other apartments. She hadn't bothered asking why.

It took from dawn until dusk to move the furniture and boxes in, then unpack enough to be ready for the following day. She set her bed up squarely beneath a lightbulb that dangled from the ceiling with a long pull chain attached.
As the sun set, the mood of the apartment transformed. The rooms that had seemed bright and cheery enough now looked bleak and eerily still, almost menacing. She went to the front door and locked the deadbolt, then the chain.

Mira checked the window locks just to be sure, then turned out all the lights except the one in the bedroom.

She lay in bed and read for a bit, trying not to think about how alone and scared she felt in the ancient apartment instead of her comfy old room at home. She finally closed her book, pulled the covers over her, then reached up and turned out the light.

As she lay on her back trying to sleep, she heard the faintest scraping sounds, barely audible. Mira strained her ears in the darkness, listening hard. There it was again. It sounded like leaves rustling inside of the walls.

Something dropped onto the bed. She felt movement across her neck and sat up. Letting out a scream, she flailed blindly at the intruder. She couldn't tell if she swatted it, and frantically reached up to turn the light on.

When Mira jerked the chain in a panic, the light fixture on the ceiling ripped out of place, swinging to the side. Hundreds of centipedes came pouring out of the hole, raining down on her from their nest as she kicked and screamed in the darkness.

The Commute

Amber was speeding to work in her little hatchback car. Her coworker Elise was in the passenger seat. They were zipping along the backroads, but they got stuck behind an old, slow moving pickup truck.

The road was curvy and treacherous for dozens of miles, and they couldn't find anywhere to safely get around it. Both girls were frustrated by how slow they were moving because they were late, and Amber began flashing her headlights. The driver of the truck didn't notice or didn't care. She began honking her horn, too, but the truck continued at the same speed.

When a short stretch of straight road opened up, Amber sped around the pickup, yelling awful insults out the window. She nearly collided with it, then narrowly missed the guardrail when she overcorrected her steering. All the while, the truck maintained its speed and course.

The girls continued down the road for a bit and came to a railroad crossing. There was a freight train barreling down the tracks in front of them, and they stopped at the flashing signal.

As they chatted impatiently, along came the pickup truck. It was moving so slowly and steadily that the girls didn't notice it until it rammed into the back of their car. The car lurched forward and they shrieked, disoriented from the impact. By the time they realized their car was still moving, they were only feet away from a thousand tons of thundering steel, and inching closer by the second.

Amber threw the car in reverse and floored the pedal, but it was no use against the heavy truck; they continued creeping closer and closer as her spinning tires smoked, smearing black rubber along the roadway. They were now inches away from certain death and still moving. Both girls were screaming as the last train car whipped past, and they were pushed onto empty tracks.

The pickup carried on, shoving their car out of the way and slowly continuing down the winding road as if nothing had even happened.

The Roommate

Joey's parents went out of town, and he was spending the weekend at his grandma's apartment in the city. She spent all her time in her wheelchair in the living room, watching tv.

The apartment was dim and musty, and Joey felt uneasy there. He found himself staring at all the little cracks and holes in the plaster walls with the sensation he was being watched. There were rustling sounds and occasional thuds. He would have sworn that the place was haunted, except he didn't believe in ghosts.

"Did you hear that, grandma?" he asked when there was a noise.

"Hear what, Joey?" she'd reply every time.

That night Joey climbed into the bed in the spare room. He lay motionless for hours, unable to sleep in his strange new surroundings, but eventually managed to doze off.

At around midnight he awoke to a dark shadow moving through the room. There was a click, followed by the slightest creak, then some rustling. He listened closely, trying to understand what he was hearing. A floorboard began to groan like someone was putting their weight on it.

"Grandma?" said Joey, and the sound stopped. He waited for a reply, fear gripping him

as no one answered.

When he turned on the bedside lamp, it revealed only an empty room. Joey looked all around but found nothing. He searched under the bed, too, yet the source of the noise eluded him. Then he checked the closet.

The bulb was burnt out, but there was no closet door, so a bit of lamplight made it in. Joey felt around and came across a tiny hook latch. When he lifted it, there was a familiar click.

A small hidden door swung toward him on

a concealed hinge that let out the slightest creak. The panel opened into total darkness, and Joey strained to see.

The floorboard groaned loudly again, and out of the hole leaned a haggard man with his finger pressed to his lips. He was filthy, and his bulging eyes were piercing and intense.

"Shhh," said the stranger in a slow, hoarse whisper as he disappeared back into the darkness. "Go back to sleep, Joey."

"Best Friends"

Jill and Amber were always together but they weren't exactly friends. All they did was bicker and fight. They were each jealous of the other, and both could hold a grudge forever. They seemed to enjoy having the other around to treat poorly and sabotage. This went on for years.

Then one day they went missing. The town organized search parties and scoured the woods for miles. There was no trace of either of them, as if they had simply vanished. After a week of searching on foot everyone was exhausted and the rescue effort was finally called off.

Another week passed, and a call came in at the local police department. The man on the line was frantic. He said there was somebody trapped underneath an ice box at the local dump.

Apparently, the girls had been playing around there, and managed to tip an unsteady refrigerator on top of themselves during one of their regular shoving matches, trapping them inside.

When the rescue crews lifted the fridge, they couldn't believe the scene before them. There sat one of the girls, filthy, but looking perfectly healthy and well-fed. The other was just a pile of clothes and bones.

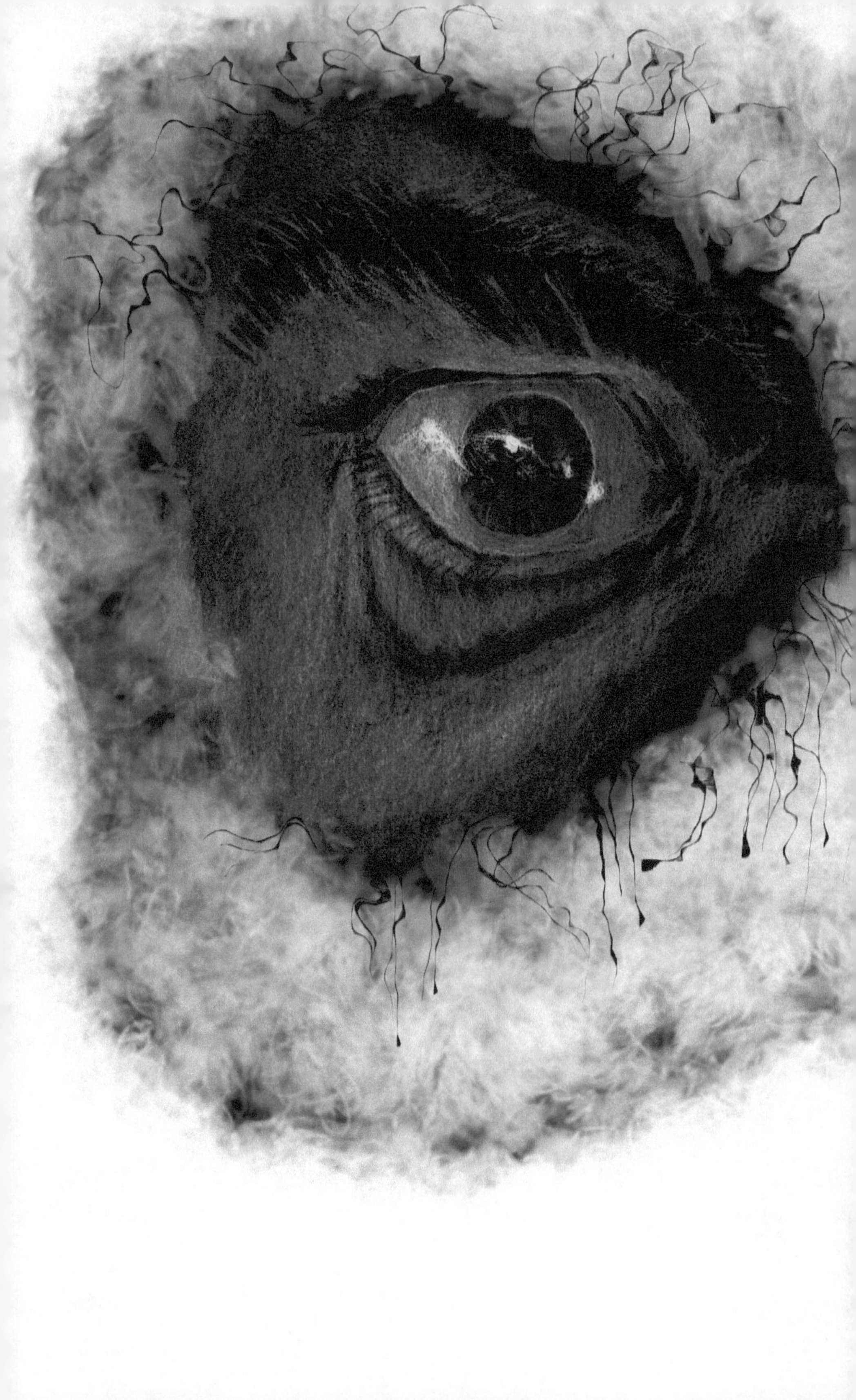

They Can See You

Act natural, don't panic. Don't turn around- they're right behind you.

Intelligent Creatures

Colby worked as a hand on a hog farm, and he did not like it one bit. For one thing, the smell was terrible. It drifted for miles around. He could even smell it at his house. The worst part was the odor stuck to you, and it was nearly impossible to wash it off.

Every day he would work himself up into a sour mood over the stench, and the filth, and he would take it out on the hogs. He'd yell at them, pour the buckets of slop right onto their heads, throw rotten vegetables at them, and occasionally he'd try to kick them as they ran past.

One day, when Colby was being particularly cruel, he noticed there was one hog watching his every move. All the others trotted, rooted, and scrambled around for the mounds of slop and random bits. They all but ignored him as they made their way, but this hog sat completely still, facing Colby, just staring at him. Colby felt like he was being judged, and it made him angrier than usual.

"Quit staring at me!" he yelled at the hog, throwing an apple core from his bucket. It hit the ground harmlessly in front of the hog, which sat motionless. Its eyes glanced down to the apple core, then back to Colby. The hog's gaze was menacing, and Colby avoided it, returning to his work.

All week it went on this way, with the hog calmly tracking his every movement on the farm, and Colby becoming increasingly agitated. He threw things, yelled insults, and made threats to the hog. It sat like a statue and stared, unimpressed. Colby's anger was seething, and he kicked a fencepost as hard as he could.

He didn't see the nail sticking out of it, and struck it dead-on. Intense pain shot through his toe as the nail pierced his boot, and he screamed. Hopping around, he gripped the injured foot tightly in his hands. He leaned his back against the gate to balance himself and get a look at his injury.

Before he could even pull off his boot, something big grabbed him from behind. It took him by the belt and jerked him into the fence with

such force he came off his feet. Dragged left and right between the posts like someone ringing a giant dinner bell, he felt like a ragdoll, utterly helpless to stop the powerful attack.

Colby was released and felt himself sailing through the air. He tumbled face-first onto the ground in a crumpled heap and lay there for a long moment.

When he finally regained his bearings, the big hog was sitting far off in the middle of the yard, staring plainly, as if nothing had happened. Colby rose slowly, dusting himself off. He hobbled back to work, and finished what would turn out to be his last shift ever.

There was security camera footage of Colby limping into a nearby convenience store. The clerk said he came in for aspirin, but turned around and left when he couldn't pay because his wallet was missing. He complained that his money and driver's license were in it, and mentioned being attacked by a hog. That was the last time anyone saw Colby Brannigan alive.

The investigation into his disappearance turned up few leads. The official report stated that someone broke in through his basement window under the cover of night, made their way up the stairs, and smashed the door to pieces. A violent struggle ensued.

It looked like a raging bull had run through the house. A trail of physical evidence was found from floor to ceiling in the bedroom, the hallway, through the dining room, all the way to the shattered sliding glass door. It continued outside onto the lawn. There, on the trampled ground, right where there should have been a body, was Colby's wallet and nothing else.

The Gogkin

If you're reading this about me it's already far too
late-
To know of my existence is to seal your worldly
fate.
I come for those who think a thought of me inside
their brains,
I get in close behind them while they wonder about
my name,
And those who turn around to show themselves
that I'm not real,
Will find they're face to face with me, quite ready
for my meal…

Crunch. Crunch. Crunch.

Adam was in his backyard setting up a tent with his best friend, Eric. The yard was just on the edge of a national forest that stretched for hundreds of miles. The old man next door saw what they were doing and called them over to the fence.

"I hope you boys aren't planning on sleeping out here overnight. This forest is a dangerous place after dark," he said, pointing to the woodline.

"We know there are bears and wolves out there. We're not scared," Adam replied.

The old man leaned in close.

"When I was a young man, a group of us went out camping in this very forest, not far from here. We were all strong lads back then, and we'd planned to spend five days out there roughing it. We didn't make it past the first night. Each of us were awakened at different times by voices we recognized, belonging to people who weren't even there. Voices asking to be let inside the tent. Bill Treader, whose family had lived here for generations, said his grandfather told stories of a shapeshifting creature that stalked the darkness, feeding on flesh and bones. It pretends to be someone you know to gain your trust, and once you invite it in, you're done. It was that grandfather's voice he heard outside our tent, but his grandfather had been dead for years. We abandoned the campsite at first light. In all the decades since then, I've never stayed in these woods past dark."

"Adam, sweetie, dinner is ready!" his mother called from the back porch.

"You might want to rethink your sleeping arrangements," the old man said, as the boys hurried into the house.

After dinner, as they were gathering their blankets, pillows, and flashlights, Eric asked, "Do you think that old man was serious?"

"Are you kidding?" Adam replied. "That guy is crazy. I've been camping before and it's a ton of fun. He's just trying to scare us."

"Have you been camping in this forest?"

"Well, no, but we're not even in the forest. We're in my backyard. It's safe."

"Yeah," Eric said. "I guess you're right."

They hunkered down in their tent as daylight faded into darkness. They told scary stories, traded jokes, and played cards until their eyelids were heavy. As they settled into their sleeping bags, the sounds of the night surrounded them. Insects buzzed noisily, droning on and on, and the boys fell fast asleep.

Adam awoke to total silence. Not a single

bug was to be heard. Then there were footsteps on the leaves.

Crunch. Crunch. Crunch.

He shook Eric awake and whispered, "Do you hear that?"

Crunch. Crunch. Crunch.

Eric didn't have to answer; there was definitely something walking around outside their tent.

The footsteps continued moving around them. The boys were gripped with absolute fear at what might be on the other side of that thin material. They became dreadfully aware of how little protection their shelter offered. A twig snapped in front of the tent and the footsteps stopped. The boys were shaking.

"Adam, sweetie, are you okay in there?" said his mother's voice, full of concern.

Adam breathed a deep sigh of relief. "Mom, you scared the heck out of us!"

"I'm so sorry, sweetie. Can I come in?"

"Yes." Adam said, without thinking twice.

When the tent flap opened, the two boys screamed.

Crunch. Crunch. Crunch.

I Wonder...

There's something in the cornfield…
It's stalking through the rows.
It started eating field mice,
But it soon moved on to crows.
It kept on growing bigger, still,
So now it don't eat those.
It's dining on coyote,
And occasionally doe.
I lay in bed and wonder,
Just how big it's gonna get,
Before I should be worried…
Am I on the menu next?

Don't Be Afraid

This chapter may be a bit spooky, but after what you've already read through, you'll likely consider these stories quite tame by comparison. This is a resting spot for the weary and a break for the frightened heart.

Peace and Quiet

One stormy afternoon an old man sat in his favorite chair sipping coffee. He had recently moved out of the city and into the country because he wanted a safer, quieter place to live.

As he looked out the window admiring his isolation, he noticed that the sky had turned an unsettling shade of green, and the gusty wind had all but disappeared. He became aware of a deep rumbling sound, like a freight train, quickly growing louder and louder, until it was deafening, and then BOOM! The whole house exploded in every direction, all at once.

The roof shook like the top of a giant, boiling kettle and then, with a terrible sound, it was gone. The walls flapped frantically like tattered rags, then were ripped skyward, disappearing into the clouds. Tables, lamps, picture frames, kitchen utensils, and clothes were flung every way imaginable. Everything was pulled upwards and cast into the swirling darkness roaring all around the terrified old man.

His home, there only moments ago, was now but a memory. The wind and debris battered him fiercely as he gripped the arms of his chair, gritted his teeth, and shut his eyes tightly. The legs of his heavy seat scraped along the hardwood floor. He felt himself and his chair rapidly lifting skyward, and he was pelted by wind and rain. Up and up he sailed, screaming through the thick, grey clouds as bolts of lightning flashed all about.

The roar quickly grew distant. Struck with a feeling of weightlessness, he stopped screaming and opened his eyes just long enough to see that the whole world was miles below. Terrified, he groaned and squeezed them shut again.

Then came the fall; his heart jumped into his throat and his stomach twisted into a knot as he began plummeting back towards the earth. He had no control and nothing to hold onto except his old armchair.

The freak storm that passed over the town had spawned a tornado. A local farmer reported he'd heard yelling and looked up in time to see someone in a chair careening far overhead, off into the distance. That was the last anyone ever saw of the old man.

No one knew for sure what became of him, but many swear he eventually landed someplace nice, upright in his chair, and the whole house fell back down around him piece by piece, good as new. Others say he's still up there to this day, stuck in a low orbit, and his wailing cries of despair can still be heard in the midwestern United States on

the first Wednesday of each month as he passes
by…

The Mortician's Apprentice

A man named Jim got a job working as a mortician's apprentice. On his first week, while embalming a corpse, the mortician told him, "This is not a job for the faint of heart, Jim. It cannot simply be taught through a textbook; it must be learned from experience. Death is a great mystery, so naturally it can be very confusing." He handed Jim a clipboard and pointed at it. "Always know the full name, place of death, and cause of death for everybody you work with, because you can't expect them to remember."

Jim took this as colorful humor, but he did as he was told, for a time. After months of work preparing countless corpses for visitation, day-in, day-out, Jim thought he was doing well just remembering their names. He wasn't sure why he needed to remember the rest, so he simply didn't.

Late one night, as Jim was busy working on a large man's funeral makeup, he switched on the overhead lamp and the body suddenly sat upright in the casket. It turned its head, and looked directly at Jim with lifeless, withered eyes. Jim almost jumped out of his skin as the corpse whispered, "Who are you?"

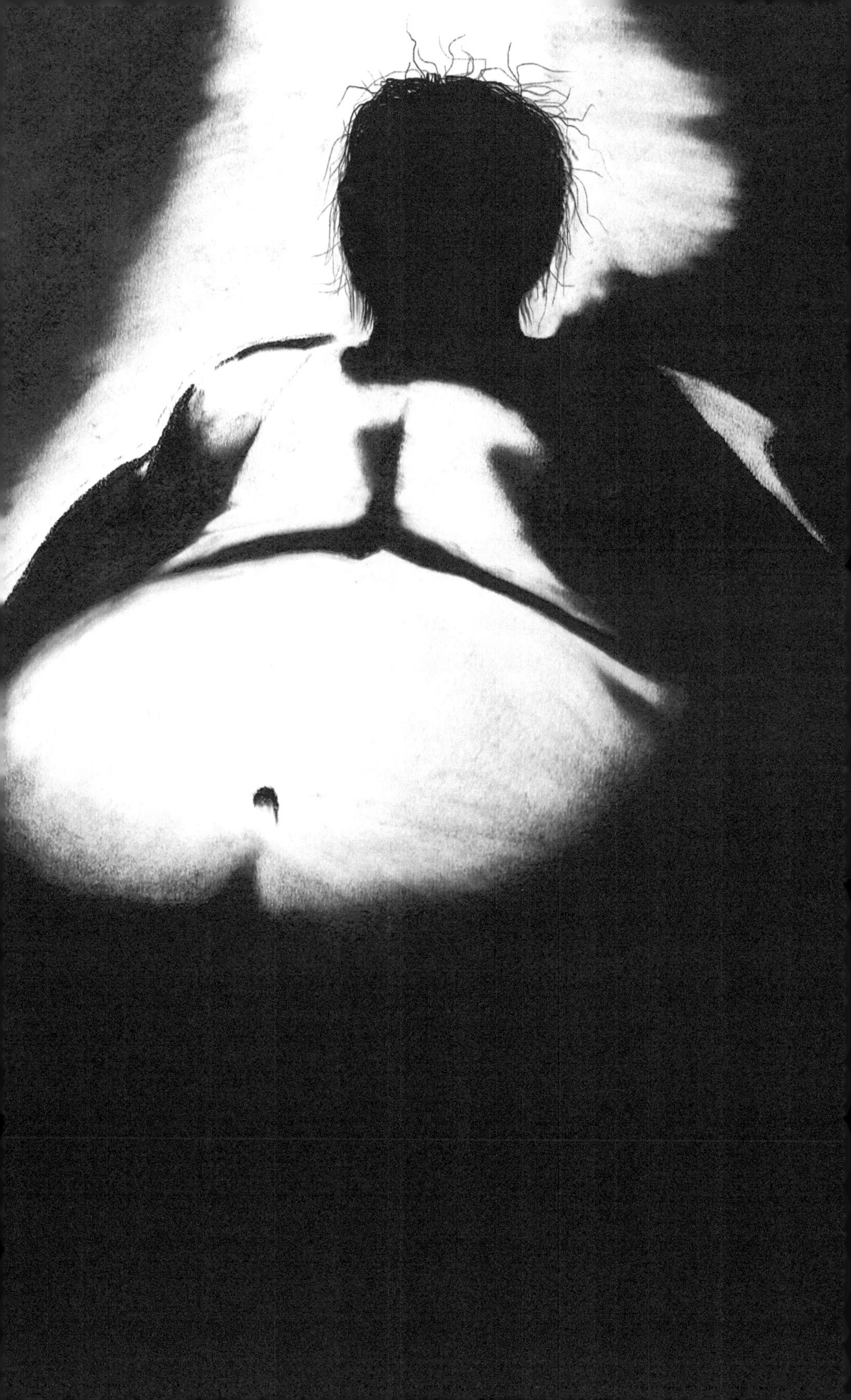

"I- I'm the m-m-mortician's apprentice," he stammered. "I'm just getting you ready for your funeral."

"I'm not DEAD!" it said, rising from the coffin and casting a looming shadow over him.

The eyes seemed to stare straight through Jim. He was terrified and didn't know what to do.

"I'm sorry, but you *are* dead."

"NO!" the corpse yelled, pounding a pale, bluish fist on the embalming cart, sending syringes, small brushes, and containers flying to the floor.

Jim wanted to cry. He wanted to run but he was frozen with fear. He felt as if he were living inside of a nightmare and couldn't wake up.

"Grady," the mortician's voice unexpectedly called out from behind Jim, who turned to look. "Your name is Michael Grady." He stepped into the room and closed the door behind him, staring at the corpse.

The dead man removed his fist from atop the cart and stood listening now.

"Two days ago, on your way home from work, your car slid off the bridge and into the river. You did not survive, Michael. You drowned."

For a time, all three stood motionless. The hum of the electric light was the only sound. Finally, the corpse groaned and stiffly returned to his coffin, satisfied with the explanation.

"I'll tell you again, Jim- no matter how it happens, the dead have been through a lot, and it's our job to help them navigate the process."

The House of Ash

The moon sits waiting as the clouds creep by,
Through the darkness, hanging in the midnight
sky.
All the twigs go *snap!* Underneath your feet,
While the dead woods chatter like a skeleton's
teeth.
In the pale moonlight, through a swirling mist,
Like a madman grinning, is a crooked iron fence.
Through the rusted gate, down a cobblestone path,
Is the crumbling wreckage of the House of Ash.

They say an old woman who was rich in things,
Once lived all alone with the sorrow that brings,
So she filled every room with what money could
buy,
But no matter what she bought, she was empty
inside.
A stray spark was all it took, and all her things fed
the flames,
While they trapped her in the house on that terrible
day.
With nobody there to help, or to hear her screams,
She shared the fate of those useless things.

Holiday ~~Cheer~~ Fear

Halloween can make us scream,
But Christmas can, as well,
When things crawl from your fireplace,
That down the chimney fell.
Even spring is quite a thing,
As Easter speaks of tombs,
And giant rabbits stalk the dark,
to sneak into your room.

With all the things your parents promised,
Into your house creep,
*How is anyone around here **getting any sleep**!?*

On The Eve

In late October winds blow colder,
Crackling fires spit and smolder,
Darkness creeping ever closer,
Steps behind you, check your shoulder.
Nothing there, is it just fear?
Still, there's footsteps growing near…
You're alone and someone laughs,
Now you're running,
Running *fast*.
Winded soon, you stop to breathe.
Something runs out from the trees,
And the last thing that you hear?
A voice screams…

…HAPPY HALLOWEEN!

A New Year

Mitchell Elliot had just gotten his license and was driving home from a friend's New Year's Eve party a few towns away. Since the journey was long, he left a half hour before midnight. To save a few minutes, he avoided the interstate that brought him there and took a shortcut down backroads he found with his GPS.

He had never been out this way before, through vast fields and rolling hills. He was passing a tattered old town with ancient trees and decrepit buildings awash in the dim glow of moonlight. The digital display on the dashboard read 11:59 as a thick fog came rolling in. It swallowed the town, the road, and the car just as the clock rolled over to midnight.

He couldn't see past his own headlights anymore and began slowing. The twisted branches and massive trunk of a tree materialized from the ghostly swirls in front of him. He jerked the wheel at the last second to narrowly avoid hitting the tree and the car skidded to a stop. His knuckles were pale from his deathgrip on the steering wheel.

After a moment he looked at the GPS, but

there was no signal, and no roads on the screen. The whole world seemed an impenetrable wall of eerie, hanging mist. Mitchell sat considering what he should do, looking down at his phone.

Something crashed onto his roof with such force that the whole car bounced. The loud clang surprised Mitchell, who cried out in panic. When he saw what made the sound he nearly jumped out of his skin; a wild-eyed man clutching a pitchfork was beside the car, readying to swing again. Mitchell screamed and the man yelled "Something dwells within!", then dropped the pitchfork while running into the fog.

Several lights appeared from the direction he'd fled, and Mitchell heard men's voices. Lanterns and torches emerged along with the figures holding them. They were dressed in dark wool, with brimmed hats and tall boots. Armed with axes, spades, and pitchforks, they looked at the car with fear and astonishment. One man uttered a prayer, clasping his hands together before him.

"This is the work of the devil himself!" cried another man, as he charged the car with an axe.

Mitchell shifted into reverse and hit the gas. The axe missed the hood by inches and plunged into the ground. The other men charged but their desperate, wide-eyed expressions and frantic

shouts quickly disappeared into the mist as Mitchell drove his car backwards to escape.

Suddenly he was outside the fog, watching it retreating as quickly as it came. As the grey wall rolled away, the wreckage of the long-abandoned town was laid out before Mitchell. He saw the men's torchlights approaching in the mist, but the fog's edge passed over them and no one was revealed, as if they all simply disappeared. There wasn't a soul in sight.

He looked at his phone and his service had returned; his GPS was back online. Mitchell drove home in shock and promptly went to bed.

The next morning, he was sure he had simply dreamed the whole thing, but when he walked outside, the roof of his car had the imprint of a pitchfork in it, plain as day.

Easter Vacation

The Gonner family were on a road trip to Embry Lake, dad's favorite spot, for a weeklong Easter vacation. Embry lake was tucked in the mountains where few people traveled. Deep, cold, and clear, it was surrounded by green alpine forests.

That summer was unusually hot, and the water temperature was warmer than their father had ever seen it. He took them to the burnt-out ruins of a small settlement on the edge of the lake and told them about the townspeople who had once lived there. He explained how they had been awful to the area's natives, and how those natives had retaliated one Easter Sunday by attacking the chapel they were gathered in and setting fire to their village. Surrounded by enemies and towering flames, the townspeople fled into the lake trying to swim to safety, but instead they drowned in the freezing waters.

After exploring, the Gonners ate a picnic lunch on the shore. The day kept getting hotter, so they decided to take a swim in the lake. As they splashed and played in the cool, deep water, the daughter's leg kicked something bulky, and a man's corpse floated up next to her. As she screamed, more bodies began popping up all around, bobbing in the water.

The horrified family called the police. Investigators came and concluded that the bodies were, in fact, the drowned villagers. The cold, deep waters had perfectly preserved them, but the rising temperatures forced their decomposition, and the resulting gases brought them up from the depths for the first time in over a hundred years.

The Final Chapter

Ah, you've made it to the final chapter. It appeared so far away when you began, and seemed to take forever to reach, but now its arrival feels abrupt, does it not? Inevitably it comes, concluding our strange journey together. I hope you've enjoyed your time and have made all your arrangements. If not, well, it's not your problem anymore, now is it?

Don't Waste Time

On his way home from school Charlie passed through a graveyard. It was dead quiet, and he soon became aware of a second set of footsteps echoing his own. He looked back to see who was following him, but no one was there.

Charlie continued on his way until he heard the footsteps again, only this time they were much closer. Charlie took off at a sprint, but something held onto his bookbag. He panicked and ran as fast as he could, but he was running in place, going nowhere. He was lifted by his backpack and carefully spun around.

He found himself face to face with a massive skeleton dressed in a flowing, black robe. In one bony hand it wielded a large scythe with a great, curved blade, the tip of which was hooked upon Charlie's bookbag. Dangling, he gazed into the grinning skull's empty sockets, and screamed. The Reaper steadily drew him in closer, slowly raising his skeletal hand between both of their faces.

"You dropped this," said Death, holding up a yellow number two pencil. His voice was

like thunder echoing through the valley. Charlie fainted.

When he awoke moments later, the skeleton was gone. The gravedigger was approaching from across the cemetery, calling "Hey, you'd better get home, to the people who love you. Go on, move like you mean it, before it gets you!"

Charlie was still stunned, and sat staring for a moment, before saying, "Wow, that was close."

"Closer than you think," said the Gravedigger, glancing over his shoulder nervously, "so you'd better hurry along. Don't forget your pencil."

Acknowledgements

To Schwartz, Gammell, Silverstein, Sendak, The Berenstains, Dahl, Poe, Crichton, King, and Saul, my sincerest thanks.

The written word was my refuge from the time I could read. From spooky old trees to wild things. Where sidewalks end, to chimneys and heads, and all that lay beyond. I'm grateful for the excitement, the joy, the humor, the lessons, the comfort, and simply the opportunity to journey into the unique interiors of your minds.

I could name countless other amazing talents who have supplied these things since, but those named here have a common thread. These artists created the words and imagery that not only first moved me to love horror as a child, and not only to love reading in general throughout my entire life, but who directly inspired me to write and illustrate this book.

Shout out to Rikk Wolf of AgonyWolf Media, all the Coggers, and my fellow "executives".

Last but not least, thank you to my amazing wife for all the love and support. I couldn't have done this without you.

www.ingramcontent.com/pod-product-compliance
Lightning Source LLC
Chambersburg PA
CBHW020119310726
48970CB00002B/703